Dream Jumper

Written by John R. Green

Illustrated by Susan Shorter

Archway Publishing books may be ordered through booksellers or by contacting:

Archway Publishing
1663 Liberty Drive
Bloomington, IN 47403
www.archwaypublishing.com
1 (888) 242-5904

Illustrations by Susan Shorter.

ISBN: 978-1-4808-9537-9 (sc)
ISBN: 978-1-4808-9538-6 (hc)
ISBN: 978-1-4808-9539-3 (e)

Printed in the United States of America.

Archway Publishing rev. date: 9/29/2020

To
Anthony,
Francesca,
and
A.J.,
who fill my heart
with love

When it's Francesca's
time to go to bed,
She'd rather do anything
else instead,

Like play with her dolls
or color a book.
She'd even rather stay
up and cook.

You see, Francesca
doesn't like to sleep.
In fact, it often
makes her weep.

Even when Dada
leaves on a light,
Bedtime always gives
her a fright.

"**I**'ll miss you so much when
I close my eyes.
Please don't leave,"
she says, and then cries.

Dada tells her, "There's
no reason to fear,
For I have a secret that
I have held dear.
Dada can magically
jump into dreams.
I'll join you in yours—
not as hard as it seems."

"Just imagine a dream you
think would be fun,
And when I go to sleep,
it will be done."

"I'll jump into your dream,
and we'll be together,
Flying on a unicorn, as
light as a feather."

She asks, "Can we slide down a rainbow too? Into a pool of teddy bears—me and you?"

"Or maybe we'll ride in
a boat on the lake,
With pizza for lunch
and a giant cupcake!"

"If that's what you want
to dream, my dear,
Then I'll jump right in—
no reason to fear.
With dreams of fun and
happy times only,
When Dada jumps in,
you'll never be lonely."

"So close your eyes. Here's
a kiss you can keep.
I'll see you again when
you fall asleep."

Acknowledgments

Many thanks to Lori Greiner for your friendship, and for encouraging me to write this book.

To Robin Roberts, Samantha Chapman and Gabriel Kerr for your incredible support and enthusiasm.

To my 1st grade teacher Christine Williams, who nurtured my passion for reading and writing at Old Bonhomme Elementary School in St. Louis.

To Anthony La Bate for your patience and creativity.

And to Francesca and A.J. for inspiring me to DREAM big.

What Dream Would You Like to Jump Into?
(Color it Here)

About the Author

John R. Green is a multiple Emmy and Peabody Award winning television news and documentary writer and producer. He is a 25 year veteran of ABC News and currently serves as Executive Producer of Special Programming there, as well as Executive Vice President of Rock'n Robin Productions, a full service production company based in New York City. In addition to writing his first kids' book *Dream Grabber* based on real bed time rituals he created to help his own young children face their bedtime fears, Green authored *Dream Jumper*, a companion book for parents and children. Green and his husband Anthony live in suburban New Jersey with their twins Francesca and A.J.

Learn more at TimeToDreamBooks.com